main road to town

the path

DISCARDED

circle of pines

berry patch

The
WOODS

trout pool

beaver lodge

railroad tracks

HOME
IN THE
WOODS

Eliza Wheeler

 Nancy Paulsen Books

For the Banks Family:
my grandma Marvel, her brothers and sisters, and their mum.

NANCY PAULSEN BOOKS
an imprint of Penguin Random House LLC, New York

Nancy Paulsen Books is a registered trademark of Penguin Random House LLC.

Visit us online at penguinrandomhouse.com

Library of Congress Cataloging-in-Publication Data
Names: Wheeler, Eliza, author, illustrator. | Wheeler, Eliza. Title: Home in the woods / Eliza Wheeler. Description: New
York: Nancy Paulsen Books, [2019] Summary: During the Great Depression, six-year-old Marvel, her seven siblings, and
their mother find a tar-paper shack in the woods and, over the course of a year, turn it into a home. Based on the author's
grandmother's childhood; includes historical notes. Identifiers: LCCN 2019008905 | ISBN 9780399162909 (hardback) |
ISBN 9780698172418 (ebook) | ISBN 9780698172425 (ebook) Subjects: | CYAC: Family life—Fiction. | Poverty—Fiction. |
Single-parent families—Fiction. | Depressions—1929—Fiction. | United States—History—1919–1933—Fiction. |
BISAC: JUVENILE FICTION / Historical / United States / 20th Century. | JUVENILE FICTION / Social Issues /
Homelessness & Poverty. | JUVENILE FICTION / Nature & the Natural World / General (see also headings under Animals).
Classification: LCC PZ7.W5623 Hom 2019 | DDC [E]—dc23 | LC record available at https://lccn.loc.gov/2019008905

Manufactured in China by RR Donnelley Asia Printing Solutions Ltd.
ISBN 9780399162909
10 9 8 7 6 5 4 3 2 1

Design by Eileen Savage. Text set in Gloucester Old Style.
The illustrations were created with dip pens, India ink, watercolors, acrylics, and pastel pencils.

This is my family.

Ray (14)

Rich (10)

Bea (12)

Marv (8)

Mum (34)

This is me.

Eva
(3 mo.)

Dal (2)

Lowell (4)

Marvel (6)

Dad lives with
the angels now,
and we need to
find a new home.

SUMMER

Deep in these woods, we find a shack
all wrapped in tar paper.
It's hot outside, but the shack
looks cold
and empty,
like I feel inside.

"You never know what treasures
we'll find," says Mum.

In the shack, we don't see any treasures.

rusty oven

dusty shelf

empty crates

potbelly stove

wooden table

box springs

But Lowell and Eva find a door in the floor.

Below is a root cellar
filled with old glass jars,
a tin pail,
a pile of rags,
and a pitcher pump that goes
up and down,
up and down,
and out comes a stream
of cool, clear water.

"This place will do fine," says my big brother Ray.
But it doesn't seem like much of a home to me.

Outside, the ground is a blanket of
rotting leaves.
Dal and Bea dig underneath to find
   soft,
        dark,
            rich soil.

"The seeds from our old garden
can go here," says Bea.

When the crystal rains fall,
our seeds slowly take root.
"Some treasures take a
little time," says Mum.

The
songs of
happy
frogs
echo
through
the trees.

The woods are a tangle of
birch,
poplar,
pine,
and sugar maple.

Marv finds the
secret paths of
whitetail deer
woven all around.

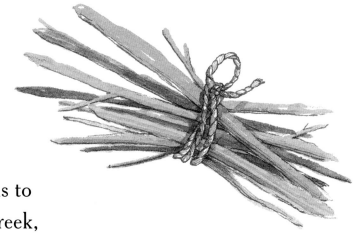

The paths lead us to
a twisting trout creek,
an empty beaver lodge,
and a blooming berry patch,
with sweet jewels of blue and red.

We fill our pail, Marv's hat, Ray's bag.
Lowell fills his empty belly.

Our
laughter
echoes
through
the
trees.

AUTUMN

Cool winds come and spice up the air
and fill it with rust and ruby leaves.

Mum walks into town to do chores for pay,
so we take care of chores at the shack.
Rich writes them on paper slips that we
draw from a hat:

split wood

pull weeds   pick veggies

hang clothes

wash up

sweep some

We fill the glass jars with
Mum's berry preserves and
the harvest from our garden.
We'll save them for winter
and stack them in the cellar
like buried treasure.

When we need more supplies, we head to Bennett's General Store.
The windows are full of marvelous things.

catalog
dresses

pearly
sweets

shiny tools

wind-up
toys

But Mum's chore money
can only buy some basics.

baking
flour

soap
flakes

lamp
oil

We say
nothing at
all on the
long walk
home.

Back at the shack, we invent a
new game—General Store.
We can buy anything we want!

Rich is
the banker.

Bea sells
fine hats.

Marv pumps gas.

Lowell is the
jeweler.

I display mud sweets.

Our
laughter
echoes
through
the trees
once
again.

WINTER

The days are dark,
and bitter winds blow.

Ray and Marv
trek out
to hunt for food.

Bea huddles in the lamp's glow.
Mum teaches her that scraps,
put together,
make colored patchwork.

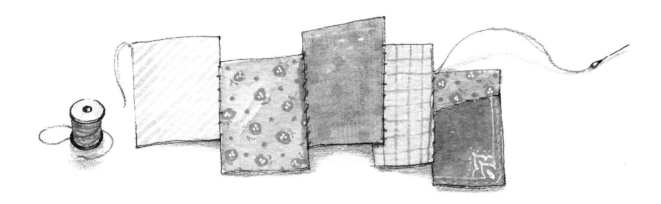

I huddle by the warm stove.
Rich teaches me that letters,
put together, make words . . .
and words, put together,
make stories.

Most days, Ray and
Marv return from
their hunt with
nothing at all,
but tonight they
are proud and tall.

We plunder our stores,
and Mum works the
oven like magic.

"A feast for the kings and queens of the forest!" Rich says.

Snow falls in a blanket of diamonds
all around the shack.
The jack pines sway above as we
fall asleep close together.
But Mum stays awake
into the night . . .

. . . whispering
to
the
stars.

SPRING

After many months, warm, fresh air
comes pouring into the shack.
The cottonwoods are all in bloom.

Me and Bea carry Mum's loaf bread and
blueberry jam to the neighbors' farm.

They fill our
pail with milk
and our hat with
golden eggs.

We go slow and careful
on the path home.
Bea calls out the flowers' names.

wood violet

dwarf iris

pink
lady's slipper

pitcher plant

The
songs of
happy
birds
echo
through
the trees.

Here in these woods,
I find my brothers, my sisters,
our mum, and me (Marvel).
The shack all wrapped in tar paper
looks different now—
warm
and bright
and filled up with love . . .

. . . like I feel inside.

Author's Note

In the fall of 1932, during the Great Depression, when my grandma Marvel was six, her family was evicted from their home in Bennett, a small town in northern Wisconsin. Her father, a munitions factory worker, began moving their belongings into an abandoned tar-paper shack deep in the woods, but he died of cancer before being able to spend a single night there.

His wife, Clara, the thirty-four-year-old daughter of Norwegian immigrants, was left to care for their eight children, ages three months to fourteen years old. With a little aid from the Mothers' Pension (an FDR program) and some janitorial work, they learned to survive mainly by growing vegetables, picking berries (she canned forty quarts of blueberries each year), fishing for trout, and hunting squirrel, rabbit, and deer. Neighbors also shared in any ways they could during those lean times. My grandma's family lived in the shack for about five years.

I grew up hearing stories of that time from my grandma Marvel—how her mother was able to make delicious food out of whatever they had; how they had to come up with their own games since they had no toys. (My grandma wants you to know that their favorite game, called "General Store" in this book, was really called "That Game.") There were stories of below-zero-degree winters made especially harsh by the weather coming off Lake Superior. My great-uncle Lowell recalled cutting firewood inside the shack on those days in order to continually feed the stove.

What an incredibly hard time it must have been, and yet they recall the memories from those years as some of their best. They all had purpose and found inventive ways to work together and make it fun. At the time of this writing, four of the eight siblings are still with us: Eva (87), Lowell (91), Marvel (93), and Rich (97).

This book is inspired not only by the stories from their childhood, but by the entire generation that experienced the Great Depression. They will soon be gone, and if we haven't yet collected their stories, the time is now.

What's your family story?
I invite you to share it with the world, and
with me, online at WheelerStudio.com.